PUFFIN BOOKS

Trouble for Alberta

Tessa Krailing was born in Kent and brought up in Sussex. She always wanted to write fiction, but started off her working life as a TV drama production secretary with the BBC, and later trained as a teacher. For fifteen years she taught mainly English and art at schools in Sussex and Switzerland, but in 1979 decided to give up teaching and concentrate on writing instead. Since then, Tessa Krailing has written over twenty books for children as well as short stories, radio and TV plays. She now lives on the Isle of Wight and is an occasional lecturer at Writers' Workshops.

TESSA KRAILING

Trouble
for Alberta

Illustrated by Jacqueline East

PUFFIN BOOKS

PUFFIN BOOKS

Published by the Penguin Group
Penguin Books Ltd, 27 Wrights Lane, London W8 5TZ, England
Penguin Books USA Inc., 375 Hudson Street, New York, New York 10014, USA
Penguin Books Australia Ltd, Ringwood, Victoria, Australia
Penguin Books Canada Ltd, 10 Alcorn Avenue, Toronto, Ontario, Canada M4V 3B2
Penguin Books (NZ) Ltd, 182–190 Wairau Road, Auckland 10, New Zealand

Penguin Books Ltd, Registered Offices: Harmondsworth, Middlesex, England

First published by Hamish Hamilton Ltd 1996
Published in Puffin Books 1998
1 3 5 7 9 10 8 6 4 2

Text copyright © Tessa Krailing, 1996
Illustrations copyright © Jacqueline East, 1996
All rights reserved

The moral right of the author and illustrator has been asserted

Filmset in Baskerville

Made and printed in England by Clays Ltd, St Ives plc

British Library Cataloguing in Publication Data
A CIP catalogue record for this book is available from the British Library

ISBN 0-140-38568 1

1. A Fishy Problem

ALBERTA COULDN'T SLEEP. It was
now three days since she had made
the long, long journey from Canada to
3b King's Villas, Cuttleworth. She
quite liked it here. She liked Felix
Dobson, the boy who lived at 3b
King's Villas, and she liked his
mother. But Cuttleworth was a very
different sort of place from the North
Pole. It had a different climate – and
that was why she couldn't sleep.

It was too darn HOT!

"It's not natural," she muttered to
herself as she tossed and turned. "I'm
an Abominable Snowthing from the

1

Arctic wastes of Canada, and I need SNOW!"

Felix had done his best. He had taken the whitest, snowiest sheet he could find and crumpled it into a nest on his bedroom floor for her to sleep in. But it didn't *feel* like snow. It wasn't cold enough. Or soft enough. Or wet enough.

Suddenly Alberta had an idea. She climbed out of the nest as quietly as she could and tiptoed over to look at Felix. He was fast asleep and snoring gently. She picked up the sheet and carried it across the landing to the bathroom.

The bathroom was lovely, all cold white tiles. She closed the door carefully so that no one could hear what she was doing, put the plug in the bath and turned on the cold tap. When the bath was half full of water

she plunged in the sheet and made it
thoroughly wet. Then she let the
water out again and climbed into the
bath to settle down. Aaaah, perfect!
Now the sheet felt soft and cold and
wet, just like snow. *Now* she could
sleep . . .

While she slept Alberta dreamed she was back home in the Arctic with her Aunt Winnipeg and Uncle Baffin and Cousin Saskatchewan. And they were fishing. "Come over here, Alberta," said Uncle Baffin. "I've made a hole in the ice specially for you." And she was just about to dip her paw into the ice-hole to pull out a slippery silvery fish when someone shook her by the shoulder and said, "Wake up, Alberta."

She opened her eyes to see Felix staring down at her. "Oh, my goodness," she said. "Is it morning already?"

"Yes, it is," said Felix, "and you'd better get out of that bath before Mum sees you."

"I already have," Mrs Dobson said, coming into the bathroom behind him. "Felix, take that sheet downstairs

and put it in the washing machine.
And when you've done that you'd
better give Alberta a rub down with
the towel to dry her off."

Alberta said quickly, "I don't need a
rub down. I'll just have a quick
shake." She shook herself so hard that
her long white hair flew out in all

directions, sending a shower of ice-
cold water over Mrs Dobson. "There,
now I look beautiful again."

Mrs Dobson wiped the spray from
her eyes. "And I look like a drowned
rat!" She snatched a towel from the
rail and marched back into the
bedroom.

"You'd better be careful, Alberta," Felix warned, "or Mum might send you to Melford Zoo after all."

Melford Zoo was where Alberta had been meant to go when she was shipped to England in a large wooden crate, but there was a mix-up over the labels and she was delivered to Felix instead.

"The Mum lady would never put me into such a horrible place," Alberta

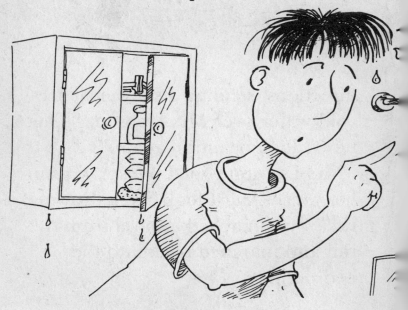

said confidently. "Not now she's seen it. She said I can stay here until you go to visit your father in Canada."

"She could change her mind," Felix warned. "Now move out of the way and let me get washed. It's nearly time for breakfast."

"I suppose," Alberta said hopefully, "there wouldn't be any chance of some fish?"

"I expect Mum would grill you a

kipper if you asked," Felix said.

Alberta had already tried a kipper. It tasted dry and smoky, quite unlike any fish she'd ever caught in the Arctic Ocean. "No, thanks," she said with a sigh. "I don't think I'll bother."

At breakfast Felix said, "Now Alberta, today's Monday. That means Mum will be at work and I've got to go to school, so you'll have to stay here on your own – and for goodness sake, try to be sensible."

"Can't I come to school with you?" she asked.

"No, that would be dangerous. If Mr Peabody saw you he might get suspicious again."

Mr Peabody was Felix's headmaster. He had already seen Alberta twice, and been very suspicious indeed. On the first occasion he was sitting in Mrs Dobson's surgery having his tooth

drilled when he caught sight of a small white furry creature dancing around outside. He was so shocked that he fainted. The second time he had spotted her on their visit to the zoo and chased them into the car park.

"Oh, all right," Alberta said reluctantly. "I'll maybe just go out for a little walk."

"No!" said Felix, horrified. "Whatever you do, you mustn't go outside the front door. People here aren't used to seeing Abominable Snowthings walking around the streets. They'd get a terrible shock."

"And try to keep out of Mrs Bassett's way," Mrs Dobson warned. "At the moment she thinks you're a girl, but if she finds out you're really an Abominable Snowthing there could be trouble."

(Mrs Bassett was the cleaning lady and very short-sighted.)

"I'll keep out of her way," said Alberta. "And I'll be really sensible, I promise."

Felix looked at her doubtfully. Being sensible was not Alberta's strong point.

She went downstairs to see him off to school. "Felix," she pleaded, "before you go . . . give me a hug!"

"Now, Alberta," Felix said sternly. 'You know I don't like being hugged, especially by you. You hug too hard. A person can't breathe."

"Oh, all right." Sadly Alberta waved goodbye as Felix went down the path. There was a lot she missed about being at home with her family, but more than anything she missed being grabbed by a pair of long furry arms and squeezed really, really tight. Aunt Winnipeg had been a wonderful hugger.

Mrs Dobson came down the stairs. "If you have any problems come and find me in my surgery," she told Alberta. Then she disappeared through a side door marked "Mrs A. Dobson, Dentist."

Any problems? Alberta sighed. She had only one problem, but it was a big one and she wasn't sure how to

solve it. She went into the living-room
and sat down on the sofa to have a
long hard think.

HOW COULD SHE GET SOME
FISH?

Real fish. Fresh fish. Delicious
slippery fish that tasted of the sea.
There must be some somewhere . . .
but where?

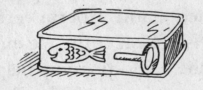

2. ASHOO!

ALBERTA WAS STILL thinking when
she heard a key turn in the front door.
Mrs Bassett!

"Keep out of her way," Mrs Dobson
had warned – and Alberta certainly
had no wish to meet the cleaning lady
again if she could possibly help it.
The last time they met Mrs Bassett
had tried to cut her lovely long silky
hair, saying it looked untidy on a girl.
She must hide!

Quickly Alberta dived over the back
of the sofa and crouched behind it,
trying to make herself as small as
possible. She heard Mrs Bassett go

into the kitchen and come out again almost at once. Then Mrs Bassett came into the sitting-room and started moving around, humming a little tune to herself. There was a sudden CRASH! as an ornament fell to the floor. She must be dusting, Alberta thought. Mrs Bassett always broke things when she was dusting.

"Ooops, clumsy me!" Mrs Bassett muttered to herself. "I'll go and fetch the dustpan and brush." And she flung the duster over the back of the sofa before leaving the room.

Alberta began to feel uncomfortable. She had been crouched in one position for some time now and longed to stretch her legs. What's more, her nose was beginning to twitch. The dust coming from the duster made her want to sneeze. Oh dear, oh dear, whatever happened she mustn't sneeze . . .

Mrs Bassett came back into the room and began sweeping the broken pieces of china into the dustpan, only a few feet away from where Alberta was hiding. Alberta tried to hold back the sneeze, but it was getting stronger and stronger at the back of her nose. Any minute now she was going to –

"ASHOO!"

Mrs Bassett stopped sweeping to listen.

"ASHOO, ASHOO!" went Alberta. Once she started she couldn't stop. "ASHOO, ASHOO, ASHOO!"

"What on earth – ?" Mrs Bassett's face appeared over the top of the sofa, her short-sighted eyes screwed up like small currants. She stared at Alberta crouched on the floor. "My, just look

at that pile of fluff! I'd better fetch the vacuum cleaner."

Alberta was horrified. She imagined being sucked up into the long dark nozzle of the vacuum cleaner and down, down into the dirty, dusty bag inside. Before she could stop herself she jumped up and said, "No! No, please don't do that!"

"Why, it's Felix's little cousin!" Mrs Bassett exclaimed. "I didn't know you were still here."

"Well, I am," Alberta said, rather crossly. She had done her best to keep out of Mrs Bassett's way, but it hadn't worked because of the sneeze. Funny, she never sneezed back home in the Arctic, even though it was so much colder there. She climbed over the back of the sofa and sat down, feeling fed up and very, very hungry.

Mrs Bassett gave her a disapproving

look. "I see you've still got all that untidy hair. It's so long it covers up your clothes."

"I'm not wearing any," said Alberta.

"What?" Mrs Bassett looked horrified. "Not wearing any clothes?"

"No, I never do." Alberta suddenly remembered how important it was that Mrs Bassett should go on thinking she was a girl. She added quickly, "Not while I'm indoors, anyway."

"Well, I never heard such a thing! You'll catch your death, going around like that."

Alberta had never heard of anyone catching death before, only fish – which reminded her of her problem.

"Mrs Bassett," she said, "could you please tell me where I can find some fish? Proper fish, I mean, not the sort that comes in a tin. Real slippery, silvery fish that smells of the sea."

Mrs Bassett thought hard. "Well, there's a wet fish shop down the High Street, on the left hand side, next to the greengrocer. You can get anything there – cod, haddock, mackerel, herrings . . ."

Alberta's mouth began to water. "I'll go and get some straight away." She ran into the hall.

"Stop!" called Mrs Bassett, following her. "You can't go out like that. You've got no clothes on."

"Oh, who cares?" Alberta said recklessly. "No one will notice."

"That's not the point," said Mrs

Bassett. "You may have a lot of hair but – but – well, it just isn't decent to go running around the streets stark naked."

Alberta hesitated. What was it Felix had said? "Don't go outside the front door. People here aren't used to seeing Abominable Snowthings walking around." But she had to go out, she

just HAD to. If she didn't have some
proper wet slippery fish to eat soon
she would starve.

"I'll try to find something to wear,"
she said reluctantly.

Mrs Bassett sniffed. "I should think
so too!"

Alberta went into Felix's room and

picked out a pair of jeans. Getting into them proved a bit of a struggle. She wasn't the right shape for jeans – her legs were too short – but at last she succeeded in doing up the zip. She looked at herself in the mirror. The jeans were a bit baggy round the ankles but never mind.

The stripy T-shirt wasn't much better. This time the trouble was her arms. They were much too long.

Alberta sighed. "There's still an awful lot of me showing," she said. "What I need is something to cover me right up."

Felix's parka jacket seemed the answer. It had a fur-lined hood she could pull up over her head so that only her face was showing. Alberta stared in the mirror again. "Now I look like one of those hungry hunters," she said. She found a pair of

Felix's trainers and put them on.
Surprisingly, they fitted quite well, but
then Abominable Snowthings have
very large feet.

Cautiously she went into the hall.
Mrs Bassett had spread newspaper
over the floor and was getting ready to
empty the vacuum cleaner bag. She
looked up at Alberta and said,
"Goodness, you're home early. I
suppose you were worried about that
little cousin of yours."

"Er, Mrs Bassett," said Alberta. "I'm not Felix."

"She's a mischief and no mistake! Wanted to go out in the street with no clothes on. Did you ever hear such a thing?"

"Mrs Bassett, it's me – Alberta. I'm wearing Felix's clothes."

"Well, seeing you're here you can give me a hand. This bag's got stuck. If you take that end and give it a tug . . ."

Alberta gave up arguing. She took the end of the vacuum cleaner bag and gave it a tug. It was stuck all right, jammed fast inside the container. She took a deep breath and tugged again, using all her strength. Suddenly . . . KER-SPLIT! The bag burst open and a cloud of grey dust exploded into the room.

Mrs Bassett gave a shriek as everything went dark.

"Ashoo!" went Alberta. The dust had started her sneezing again.

"Ashoo, ashoo, ashoo, ashoo . . . !" She couldn't stop. Before she realised what was happening she had sneezed herself across the hall and "ASHOO!" right down the stairs.

When Alberta had picked herself up she paused.

Should she tell the Mum lady she was going out? It might be awkward if

Mrs Dobson went up to the flat and discovered she was missing. But at that moment Alberta's stomach gave a loud rumble. It was no good, she couldn't bear to wait another minute.

Thank goodness she had stopped sneezing. She brushed the dust off Felix's parka and pulled the hood closely round her face before opening the front door.

3. No Money!

A FEW PEOPLE turned to stare at the strange little figure in baggy jeans and a parka, but most were too busy going about their daily shopping to take a second look. When Alberta reached the wet fish shop she had to join a queue, but she passed away the time by gazing at all the beautiful slippery silvery fish displayed on the slab. What should she ask for? The mackerel, perhaps; or that nice fat juicy piece of cod.

"Yes, Madam?" The fishmonger looked over Alberta's head to the woman standing behind her. "What

can I do for you?"

"Excuse me!" Alberta said indignantly. "It's my turn next."

"Sorry, love," said the fishmonger. "I didn't see you. Bit on the short side, aren't you?"

"I can't help that," said Alberta. "It's the way I was made."

The fishmonger stared down at her with a puzzled expression.

"Short . . . and round . . . and very,
very hairy," he muttered, half to
himself.

"My Aunt Winnipeg says it's rude to
make personal remarks," said Alberta.
"Now, may I have some fish, please?"

The fishmonger blinked. "Yes. Yes,
certainly you can," he said. "What
would you like?"

In some ways he reminded her of

Uncle Baffin. Alberta decided it must be his droopy moustache.

"I'll take some of that haddock," she said, "and six or seven herrings and that delicious-looking cod. Oh, and a dozen mackerel – no, I'd better have two dozen, just to be on the safe side."

The fishmonger looked surprised. "That's a lot of fish, love. Are you sure you've got enough money?"

"Money?" Alberta looked blank.

"Yes, money. You have to pay for it, you know."

"Oh, do I? No, I didn't know."

People behind her in the queue started to laugh.

The fishmonger asked gently, "Come from foreign parts, have you, love? Somewhere abroad?"

"Yes, I have," said Alberta, thinking he must have noticed her Canadian accent. "But I'm over here staying

with Felix Dobson and his mother at
3b King's Villas."

"Would that be Mrs Dobson the
dentist?"

"Yes, it would. She's very nice but

she doesn't keep much fish in the
house and I'm terribly hungry.
Couldn't you please let me have a
couple of herrings, just as a present?"

The fishmonger sighed. "Well now,
I'd love to give you some, I really
would. But you see, I'm in this
business to make a living. I can't

afford to start giving my fish away. If I
did that I'd go hungry myself."

Alberta cast a longing look at the
rows and rows of slippery, silvery fish
laid out on the slab. "No money, no
fish?"

"'Fraid not, love. You go and fetch
some money and then you can have as
much fish as you want. The whole
shopful if you're rich enough."

"I see," she said sadly. And then,
because he smelled so deliciously of
fish, reminding her more than ever of
Uncle Baffin, she reached across the
counter and gave him a hug. "You're a
very nice man, even if you won't give
me any mackerel. Goodbye."

"G-g-goodbye," stammered the
startled fishmonger.

Sadly Alberta left the shop. All that
lovely fish . . . and yet she couldn't
buy any because she had no money.

She supposed she should have thought of that before, but Abominable Snowthings never carried cash about with them. They had no use for it. In the Arctic fish came free.

Where could she get some money? Suddenly she had a brainwave.

Felix's school was not far from here, at the other end of the High Street. He had pointed it out to her once when they were in the car. All she had to do was find Felix and ask him for some money!

She heard the children long before

she reached the school. It was morning breaktime and they were all out in the playground, yelling and screaming and running around. Alberta climbed on to the wall and looked for Felix.

She spotted him almost at once. He was playing football with two other boys at the other end of the playground. She called out, "Felix! Felix, hallooo!", but he was too far away to hear.

"Hey, you!" said a ginger-haired girl who was standing by herself.

Surprised, Alberta looked round. "Do you mean me?"

"Yes, you. Little fat person sitting on the wall. Who are you and what do you want?"

She didn't sound at all polite. In fact she sounded rude and unfriendly.

"My name's Alberta," Alberta

replied with dignity. "And I want to speak to Felix Dobson. Please could you fetch him for me?"

"Why do you want Felix?"

"That's my business." Alberta pulled the hood of her parka even closer round her face. The way the girl was staring at her made her feel uncomfortable. Also, there was

something strangely familiar about
that ginger hair and sharp bony
nose.

"My name's Davinia Peabody," said
the girl, "and my father's the
headmaster of this school. So you'd
better tell me why you want Felix or
I'll go and fetch my dad!"

Of course! Now Alberta knew where

she had seen the girl before – at Melford Zoo, when the entire Peabody family had become suspicious and chased them into the car park. If Davinia were to recognise her . . .

"Er, I don't think I'll bother," she said hastily. "It wasn't important, anyway."

"Wait!" Davinia grabbed hold of the front of her parka. "Take off that hood so that I can see your face."

Alberta struggled to break free. "You're hurting me. Let me go!"

"Not until I get a really good look at you." With her free hand Davinia pushed back Alberta's hood. "Gosh, you're ugly!"

Alberta had never been so insulted in her life. "I'm *not* ugly!" she retorted. "I'm beautiful. My Aunt Winnipeg told me so," And with a huge effort she broke free at last from Davinia's grasp. She jumped down from the wall into the playground and ran to take cover behind the bicycle shed.

4. A Geography Lesson

"STOP! STOP, COME back," shouted Davinia; but at that moment the bell sounded for the end of break and everyone in the playground fell silent.

"Who's Davinia shouting at?" Felix asked his friend Jon as they filed back into the classroom.

"Haven't a clue," muttered Jon. As they reached the classroom he asked, "What have we got next?"

Felix looked at the timetable. "Oh, no! It's geography," he groaned, collapsing into his seat.

Geography with Mr Peabody was the worst lesson of the week. If only they

could learn about somewhere interesting like Canada, where Felix's father was working for the Forestry Commission. Or the Arctic, where Alberta came from.

Jon gave him a nudge. "Here's Davinia. Hey, watch out! I think she's coming over."

"Felix Dobson!" Davinia's voice was shrill and excited. "You have some very peculiar friends, I must say. I never saw such a weird-looking person in all my life."

"Don't know what you're talking about." Felix buried his head in his book.

"Yes, you do. You must do. We saw you together at the zoo, so you needn't pretend."

"Silence, please!" Mr Peabody entered the classroom.

If it were any other teacher Davinia

would have continued talking, but because it was her father she obeyed at once, taking her seat at the other side of the room. However, she kept giving Felix threatening looks, as if she were saving up what she had to say until later.

Felix yawned. The lesson seemed to go on and on for ever. Mr Peabody had such a boring voice, droning on

and on about the sugar-beet industry.
Felix yawned again and gazed out of
the window.

Suddenly a face appeared – then
disappeared just as quickly, as if
someone small had jumped up, trying
to look into the classroom. It was a
strange face, and yet somehow
familiar . . .

Felix leaned sideways. If he tipped

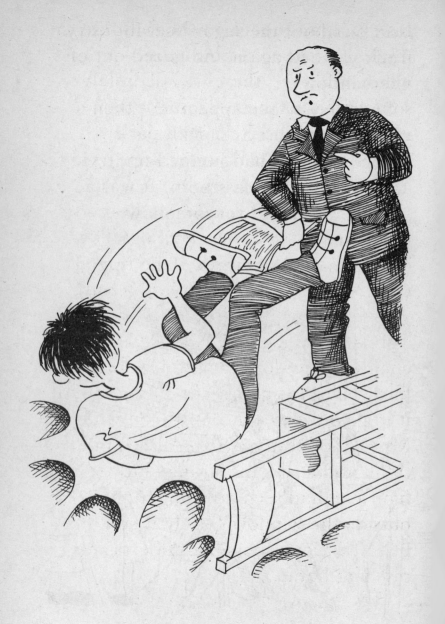

his chair far enough to the right he might be able to see over the windowsill. Yes, there was definitely somebody out there – somebody rather short and wearing a parka.

Somebody wearing *his* parka!

CRASH!

"Felix Dobson!" roared Mr Peabody. "How many times have I told you, it's dangerous to tip sideways on your chair? Serve you right if you've hurt yourself. Help him up, somebody."

Slightly stunned, Felix picked up his chair and sat down again. He wasn't hurt, just a little bruised, but he found it impossible to concentrate on what Mr Peabody was saying. All he could think about was the strange little figure he had seen creeping along outside the window. Surely it couldn't be . . . ? No, impossible! Alberta was safely at home.

Wasn't she???

Alberta heard the crash and it startled her. She thought she had seen Felix inside the classroom but she couldn't be sure, and when she heard Mr Peabody's roaring voice she decided she had better move on. She crept further along the path until she came to the next window.

Ah, this was better! Beside the window was a drainpipe and if she climbed up as far as the ledge she would be able to see inside. But although Alberta was normally an excellent climber because of her long arms, today she was hampered by her cumbersome clothes. It was quite a struggle to pull herself up the drainpipe and swing sideways on to the ledge.

She peered inside. This room was

much smaller than the classroom had
been. There was a desk, a chair, a
filing cabinet and a square wooden
table under the open window. The
desk was covered with paper, there
was a plastic cup on top of the filing
cabinet, and on the square wooden
table stood a round glass bowl
containing some water and two bright
orange . . . FISH!

Alberta stared. And stared and
stared and stared.

Yes, they were definitely fish, although she had never seen such brightly coloured ones before, and they were swimming round and round and round in the bowl, until she began to feel dizzy watching them. They looked delicious, like little golden sprats. Hardly more than a snack really, but she felt so hungry that even a snack would be better than nothing.

Alberta licked her lips. Taking care

not to lose her balance, she opened
the window a little wider.

Any minute now – and the fish
would be hers!

5. A Shock for Mr Peabody

MR PEABODY WAS glad when the geography lesson was over and he could return to his office. So far it had been a very trying day. Nobody had listened properly to his lecture about the sugar-beet industry, and that wretched boy Felix Dobson falling off his chair hadn't helped. And then earlier in the day he had caught Susie Baker trying to smuggle in two goldfish in a bowl, even though she knew that pets weren't allowed. Of course he had confiscated them and now the bowl was sitting in his office.

He opened the door and stopped, frozen with amazement.

Framed in the window was the most extraordinary figure he had ever seen. It wore baggy jeans and a parka with one sleeve rolled up, revealing a long white hairy arm – and with this arm it was reaching into the goldfish bowl, groping about in the water. Mr Peabody was about to open his mouth and shout, "Help, help, we're being burgled!", when it suddenly struck him that he had seen that long white hairy arm somewhere before . . .

"The dentist's chair," he muttered. "I saw it when I was in the dentist's chair – and then again at the zoo – and now it's come back to haunt me. Aaaaah!"

And he slid to the floor in a dead faint.

*

Felix rushed out into the playground. By now he was convinced that the strange figure in the window had been Alberta, wearing *his* parka!

"Where are you going?" asked Jon, following him. "It's dinner-time now."

"Yes, I know," muttered Felix. "But I have to find someone first."

"Who?"

"I'll explain later."

He ran round the side of the school building until he came to the window where he had seen Alberta. Now, if she'd come looking for him, where would she have gone next?

He moved cautiously along the path, aware that he was dangerously close to Mr Peabody's study. As usual the window was open – Mr Peabody was a fiend for fresh air – but who was this climbing out backwards, looking so clumsy and furtive?

"Alberta?" said Felix. "Is that you?"

"Sssh!" she hissed. "Keep your voice down or you'll wake Mr Peabody."

"What do you mean, wake Mr Peabody?"

"He's lying on the floor, fast asleep." She sat on the window ledge, her feet

dangling. "Oh, Felix! I'm so glad to see you."

"Well, I'm not at all glad to see *you*," he said sternly. "What are you doing here? And why are you wearing my clothes?"

"I was hungry," she said, as if that explained everything.

He stared at her. "You're a very odd shape. What's that huge bump inside your parka? Or rather, inside *my* parka."

"Only my lunch."

Felix's eyes narrowed suspiciously. "Show me."

With great reluctance Alberta opened the parka to reveal a glass bowl containing two very alarmed-looking goldfish.

"They're not very big." she said, "but I was so terribly hungry. I couldn't buy any fish because I didn't have any money – that's why I came looking for you – and then I saw these little orange sprats swimming around in the bowl . . ." Her voice trailed off as she saw the horrified look on Felix's face.

"They're not sprats, they're goldfish!" he said. "And they belong to

Susie Baker. Mr Peabody confiscated
them this morning. She'd be
dreadfully upset if you ate them."

"Perhaps we needn't tell her?"
Alberta said hopefully.

Felix shook his head. "Sorry, but you
can't possibly go around eating
people's goldfish. You'll have to put
them back."

Alberta's mouth quivered. "Put them back?"

"Yes. Now. Right this minute. Before you get down from that window sill."

"But – but – Mr Peabody might wake up."

Felix peered over the window sill. "No, it's all right. He's still asleep. I can see his feet sticking out from the other side of the desk." He grinned. "He must have been as bored by his geography lesson as we were."

Sadly Alberta replaced the bowl on the table. "There," she sighed, giving the goldfish one last hungry look. "Now could you help me down, please?"

Felix lifted her off the ledge and set her safely on the ground.

"You look ridiculous," he said. "I bet people gave you some funny looks."

"I didn't notice. Felix, could you give

me some money so that I can go back
to the fish shop?"

Before he could answer he heard a
voice calling, "Felix! Felix Dobson,
where are you? I know you're out here
somewhere."

"Quick!" Felix caught Alberta's hand
and pulled her along the path. "We've

got to get you away before Davinia
catches us."

When Mr Peabody eventually came to
his senses he struggled to his feet and
sank on to the chair. What had
happened? He must have fainted – but
why?

Wait, it was all coming back to him
now. Something about a burglar . . .
and a long white hairy
arm . . . and Susie
Baker's goldfish . . .
Fearfully Mr Peabody
looked at the window.

No burglar. He looked at the table. There were the goldfish swimming around in their bowl as if nothing had happened. Had he dreamed it? Was it all just a nightmare? Yes, it must have been.

"Daddy, Daddy!" Davinia burst into the room, looking red in the face and very cross. "Have you seen Felix Dobson?"

Mr Peabody made an effort to pull himself together. "Not since he fell off his chair during my geography lesson."

"I've been looking for him everywhere. And you know that white furry creature we saw him with at the zoo? Well, it was here. I saw it at breaktime, and – "

"Davinia, be quiet!" Mr Peabody rose to his feet his face like thunder. "You're talking nonsense."

"No, I'm not! I did see it."

"Impossible. Never mention such a
thing to me again. Don't mention it to
anyone, do you hear? Now go away.
No – wait!" He crossed to the table
and picked up the goldfish bowl.
"Give this back to Susie Baker and tell

her – tell her she's never to bring any
pets to school again. Understood?
Right, now GO!"

And Davinia went, clutching the
bowl and muttering to herself
something very rude about fathers
who also happened to be headmasters.

6. *In Disgrace*

"WHERE – WHERE ARE we going?"
Alberta asked breathlessly as Felix
dragged her along the High Street.

"Home," said Felix.

"But I'm still hungry!"

"So am I," he said grimly. "I'm
having to go without my lunch
because of you."

"Oh Felix, look – there's the fish
shop! Please let's stop and buy some
fish."

"You can have some fish when we
get home. I'll open a tin of sardines."

"I don't *want* something out of a
tin," Alberta protested. "I want some

lovely, slippery silvery fish, fresh from the sea and smelling of salt."

Felix didn't answer. He just went on dragging her up the High Street until they reached 3b King's Villas.

As soon as they were inside the hall Mrs Dobson appeared from her surgery. She looked rather cross. "Would someone kindly tell me what's been going on?" she demanded.

Felix tried to explain. "Alberta wanted some fish but she didn't have any money, so she came to find me at school, and, er – well, now I've brought her home."

"So I see," said Mrs Dobson in an icy voice. "But that doesn't explain the mess upstairs."

"What mess?" asked Felix.

Alberta shuffled her feet uncomfortably.

"Follow me," said Mrs Dobson, "and

I'll show you."

She started up the stairs. Felix looked sternly at Alberta.

"I don't know what you've done," he muttered, "but Mum's obviously hopping mad."

"Oh, dear," said Alberta nervously. "Do you think she'll send me back to the zoo?"

"She might do," said Felix. "We'd better go and find out."

They followed Mrs Dobson up the stairs and into the flat.

"This," she said, pointing at the hall, "is the mess I'm talking about."

The vacuum-cleaner still stood on the sheet of newspaper, and all around it lay a thick coating of grey, fluffy dust. It lay over the furniture, over the radiator, over the picture frames. Dust everywhere. You could even smell it in the air.

"Mrs Bassett left a note," continued Mrs Dobson. "I'll read it to you. It says. 'That Felix, he broke the vacuum bag and then he run off. Sorry, Madam, but I can't go on working here. There's been too much trouble lately. Yours regretfully, Thelma Bassett."

"It wasn't me," Felix protested. "I wasn't here. I was at school. It must have been . . ."

They both turned to stare at Alberta.

"I only ran off because the dust made me sneeze." she explained. "And I only went out because I was hungry."

Her stomach gave a little gurgle as if to prove she was telling the truth.

"Oh, Alberta!" sighed Mrs Dobson. "I know you don't mean to be naughty, but you just don't seem to be able to keep out of trouble. The

question is, how much more damage are you likely to do?"

Before Alberta could answer there came a ring at the doorbell.

"Felix, go and see who that is," said Mrs Dobson. "Alberta, you'd better take off those clothes – and then you can come and help me clear up this mess."

Alberta was only too glad to take off Felix's clothes. They were very hot and weighed about a ton. She shook out her long white silky hair and looked at herself in the mirror.

"That stupid girl, calling me ugly," she said to herself. "It's a good thing Aunt Winnipeg didn't hear. She'd have given her a real telling-off!"

Suddenly she felt very, very homesick. She missed Aunt Winnipeg terribly. And Uncle Baffin. And even her goody-goody cousin

Saskatchewan. Saskatchewan never
got into trouble like she did. He would
never have let himself be captured
and sent off to England in a crate –
and even if he had he wouldn't have
gone around making dust storms and
upsetting headmasters.

A tear trickled down Alberta's cheek.
She had never felt so miserable in her
life. Nobody liked her, not even Felix.

And Mrs Dobson was probably going
to send her back to the zoo, where she
would be kept inside a cage like the
poor polar bears they'd seen on their
visit.

"Alberta!" called Mrs Dobson.
"Come here, please."

She wiped away her tears and went into the hall, wondering what else she could possibly have done wrong.

Felix stood clutching a paper parcel. "That was the fishmonger at the door," he told Alberta. "He said he felt mean not giving you any fish, especially as Mum cured his toothache only last week. But he couldn't give you any in front of the other customers in case they all wanted free fish. So he sent you these as a present."

He undid the paper to reveal four silvery, slippery mackerel.

"Oh!" gasped Alberta. "Oh, how beautiful! How delicious! I've never had such a lovely present before." Then she remembered the trouble she was in and said earnestly to Mrs

Dobson. "But I won't eat them until I've cleared up the dust. And I'll tell Mrs Bassett it was all my fault and I'm sorry. I'll do anything you want, but *please* don't send me to the zoo."

Mrs Dobson sighed. "All right, as long as you promise to be good." She shook her head and smiled. "Don't worry about the dust just yet," she said. "You'd better eat those fish straight away before your stomach rumbles any louder."

"Oh, thank you!" said Alberta. "I will. But first I must thank that nice fishmonger."

"He's already gone," said Felix. "But he did ask me to give you something else."

"What's that?"

Felix looked embarrassed. "A great big hug, in return for the one you gave him."

Alberta felt almost as pleased about the hug as she did about the fish. "Come on, then," she said, flinging wide her arms.

Felix cast an appealing look at his mother. "Mum, must I?"

"Yes, I rather think you must," said Mrs Dobson, hiding a smile.

So Felix did. Or rather, he let
Alberta do the hugging because she
was much more experienced at it than
he was. She gave him one of her best
giant ribcrackers, until at last he
gasped and begged her to stop.

And then she ate the fish.